The Midnight Ride of
THOMAS THE TANK ENGINE

Based on *The Railway Series* by the Rev. W. Awdry
Illustrated by Owain Bell

This book has been printed with a nontoxic ink that glows in the dark. When you see the 🔦 symbol, turn off the lights and see what glows. Then turn the lights back on and continue reading.

RANDOM HOUSE 🏠 NEW YORK

Copyright © by William Heinemann Ltd. 1994. All rights reserved under International and Pan-American Copyright Conventions. Published in the United States by Random House, Inc., New York. All publishing rights: William Heinemann Ltd., London. All television and merchandising rights licensed by William Heinemann Ltd. to Britt Allcroft (Thomas) Ltd. exclusively, worldwide.

Library of Congress Cataloging-in-Publication Data
Awdry, W. The midnight ride of Thomas the Tank Engine / illustrated by Owain Bell. p. cm. "Based on The railway series by the Rev. W. Awdry." SUMMARY: Thomas the Tank Engine, on a midnight run to take toys to the children's hospital, has an accident and must rely on some new friends to help him complete his task. ISBN 0-679-85643-9 [1. Railroads—Trains—Fiction.] I. Bell, Owain, ill. II. Awdry, W. Railway series III. Title PZ7.A9613Mi 1994 [E]—dc20 93-26587
Manufactured in Taiwan 10 9 8 7 6 5 4 3 2 1
Random House New York, Toronto, London, Sydney, Auckland

Thomas is taking four carloads of toys to the children's hospital in the next town. He's making a midnight run so the toys will be there by tomorrow morning.

Light your headlamps, Thomas—
off you go into the night.

Peep! Peep!
There goes Thomas along the track,
Ping! Ping! Crash!
Oh, dear—some falling rocks have
broken Thomas's headlamps!

What will Thomas do without any lights? He can't run in the dark. And the children in the hospital will be so disappointed if they don't get those toys.

But look! A farmer is lending
Thomas the lamp from his barn.
That's better, isn't it!

Go slowly, Thomas. That small
lamp gives only a small light.

Luckily, some more friends
have arrived to help. 🫙
That's even better!

And the nice man
in the general store has
offered to lend Thomas
his Christmas lights.

There you go, Thomas!
Don't you look cheery!

There's the hospital in the distance.
But the tunnel lies ahead. And the
tunnel is awfully dark.

Look—Thomas has
a special escort!

Hurray for Thomas! He made it
to the children's hospital.

Thomas the Tank Engine, you've lit up the night!